P9-DXL-278

RIDER WOOFSON

LABRA-CADABRA-DOR'S REVENGE

BY WALKER STYLES **ILLUSTRATED BY BEN WHITEHOUSE**

LITTLE SIMON
New York   London   Toronto   Sydney   New Delhi

LITTLE SIMON

An imprint of Simon & Schuster Children's Publishing Division
1230 Avenue of the Americas, New York, New York 10020
First Little Simon hardcover edition February 2017
Copyright © 2017 by Simon & Schuster, Inc.
Also available in a Little Simon paperback edition. All rights reserved, including the right of reproduction in whole or in part in any form. LITTLE SIMON is a registered trademark of Simon & Schuster, Inc., and associated colophon is a trademark of Simon & Schuster, Inc.
For information about special discounts for bulk purchases, please contact Simon & Schuster Special Sales at 1-866-506-1949 or business@simonandschuster.com. The Simon & Schuster Speakers Bureau can bring authors to your live event. For more information or to book an event contact the Simon & Schuster Speakers Bureau at 1-866-248-3049 or visit our website at www.simonspeakers.com.
Designed by Laura Roode. The text of this book was set in ITC American Typewriter.
Manufactured in the United States of America 0117 FFG
2 4 6 8 10 9 7 5 3 1
Library of Congress Cataloging-in-Publication Data
Names: Styles, Walker, author. | Whitehouse, Ben, illustrator.
Title: Labra-Cadabra-Dor's revenge / by Walker Styles ; illustrated by Ben Whitehouse.
Description: First Little Simon paperback edition. | New York : Little Simon, 2016. |
Series: Rider Woofson ; 7 | Summary: After breaking out of prison, tricky magician Labra-Cadabra-Dor puts canine detective Rider Woofson under an evil spell.
Identifiers: LCCN 2016024846 | ISBN 9781481485920 (pbk) |
ISBN 9781481485937 (hc) | ISBN 9781481485944 (eBook)
Subjects: | CYAC: Mystery and detective stories. | Detectives—Fiction. | Dogs—Fiction. | Magicians—Fiction. | Magic tricks—Fiction. | BISAC: JUVENILE FICTION / Readers / Chapter Books. | JUVENILE FICTION / Action & Adventure / General. | JUVENILE FICTION / Animals / General. Classification: LCC PZ7.1.S82 Sm 2016 | DDC [Fic]—dc23
LC record available at https://lccn.loc.gov/2016024846

CONTENTS

chapter
ONE

A DOG
IN A CAGE

🐾

"I have a package for Labra-cadabra-dor from Rider Woofson," said the delivery bird. He was a nervous bird. He'd never delivered a package to a prison before, let alone to the Cage—a prison that held only the most dangerous criminals.

"We'll take it from here," one

of the prison guards said. He held the box up to his ear and gave it a little shake. "Well, it's not ticking. That's a good sign." Then the guard ran it through an X-ray machine. "Looks like we've got a cake."

"Run it through again," said the warden. "You can never be too sure when it comes to Labra.

Before he was an inmate, that pesky pup was the world's most dangerous magical criminal."

The guard ran several more tests. He even opened the box. The cake had white frosting and a bunch of candy stars that spelled out "HAVE A MAGICAL DAY!"

"Hmm, cute," said the warden suspiciously.

"The cake is safe, Boss," said the guard. "The only other thing in the box is a flimsy spoon."

The warden picked up the long spoon and examined it. "Okay, I'll deliver it myself."

He carried the cake down a series of highly protected hallways through lots of thick doors. The first door needed a card

swipe to open. The next one needed paw prints. The third door needed an eye scan, breath scan, and voice recognition. After all, the Cage was an inescapable prison.

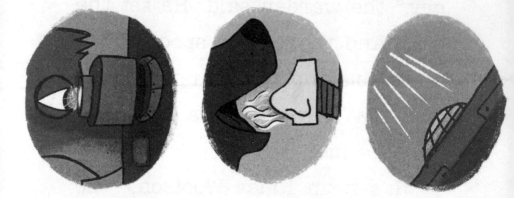

Finally, the warden arrived at the last security checkpoint. He put on a pair of special sunglasses before stepping into the cell.

Labra-cadabra-dor was sitting on his cot, reading a book. He looked kind and innocent, but the warden knew better. "Special delivery," the warden said. He set the cake and the plastic spoon down on a table and backed up slowly.

"What's this?" Labra asked. "A cake for me?"

"It's from Rider Woofson," the warden said.

"Ahh, that's right! Today is the

anniversary of when he sent me to jail," said Labra. "It's so sweet of him to remember."

The warden watched Labra carefully. "You can have one slice of the cake since it's from Detective Woofson," he said. "I'm going to watch you eat it, just in case there are any magic tricks up your sleeve."

Labra walked over to the cake and swiped a bit of the frosting into his mouth. "Vanilla. How boring. It's the *least* magical flavor." He picked up the spoon and, with a quick flick of his paw,

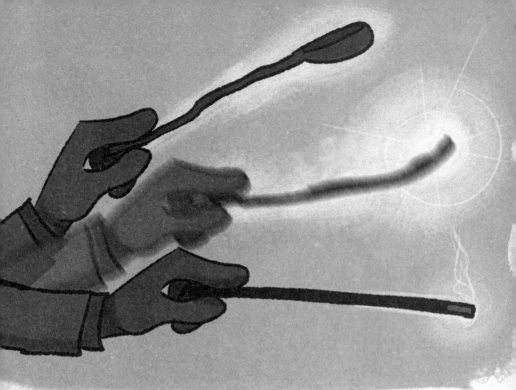

it turned into a magic wand.

"Hey! What? No!" shouted the warden, but it was too late.

"I'll take these," said Labra. With a wave of the magic wand, the special glasses flew off the

warden. Then Labra hypnotized
him. "Oh, dear, Warden. I don't
think this gift came from Rider
Woofson at all. Still, I should visit
Pawston to thank the detective—
for putting me behind bars."

HARE
OF THE DOG

Ziggy Fluffenscruff stood in the middle of the P.I. Pack office. He was wearing a cape and holding a hat. "Hey, everyone! Watch me pull a rabbit out of my hat!" The young detective reached into the hat and then lifted his paw high in the air. It was empty.

"Umm, is it an invisible rabbit,

kid?" joked Rora Gooddog. She was one of the city's most brilliant detectives.

"Well, now what did I do wrong?" Ziggy looked down into the hat.

"Hmm . . . for starters, that's *my* hat," Rider said with a smile.

"Then where's *my* hat?" Ziggy asked.

Westie Barker walked into the room wearing a top hat. He had been fixing a gadget in his lab. Slowly, the hat lifted up and a rabbit peeked out.

"Psst, Ziggy. What's my cue?" the rabbit whispered.

"Rita Rabbit!" Ziggy barked. "How'd you get over there?"

"Nice *hare*-style, Westie," Rora said.

Everyone had a chuckle, except for Westie, who didn't get the joke.

"There's a hare on your head," Rider explained.

"Of course there's hair on my head," Westie said. "I'm a dog. I'm covered in hair."

"No, they mean 'hare,' as in rabbit, as in me," said Rita. She hopped off Westie's head and onto

a desk. "Hi! I'm Rita, Ziggy's magician's assistant. And actually, I'm a rabbit, not a hare."

"Ohhhh," Westie said, still confused. He took off the hat and put

it on a desk. "Nice to meet you?"

Rita hopped back into the top hat. "Do you want to try again, Zig?" Rita asked.

"Duh!" said Ziggy. "If I want to be a magician, I need to practice!"

"Well, we all know there's no such thing as magic," Westie said. "It's all an act."

"*Bow-wowza*, Westie! You sure know how to ruin a magic trick," Ziggy said with a frown.

"What can I say?" Westie said. "I am a scientist. That means I believe in science and facts."

The phone rang, and Rider answered it. Suddenly, his face turned pale. "I see," he said. "Thank you, Mr. Mayor." Then he hung up.

"What is it, Boss?" Rora asked.

"I'm afraid I have some bad news, P.I. Pack," Rider said. "Labra-cadabra-dor has escaped. The mayor thinks he's coming to get his revenge on me."

"As in the same Labra who made Pawston City Bridge disappear?" asked Westie.

"As in the same Labra who stole Queen Elizapup's crown and scepter?" asked Ziggy.

"As in the same Labra who sawed a military plane

in half—while it was flying?!"
Rora asked.

"Yes, yes, and yes," Rider said
in a tired voice. "We all know
what Labra's done, but I'm worried
about what he's going to do next.
If Labra comes back to Pawston
for an encore act, we need to be
ready for anything."

chapter
THREE

TRICKS AND TROUBLE

"Any news, Boss?" Ziggy asked.

Rider was listening to the police scanner. "I'm afraid not. It's your typical cat-stuck-in-a-tree kind of day. What are you doing?"

"Looking online for anything out of the ordinary around town," Ziggy said, checking the computer. "If Labra shows up anywhere on social media, I'll be the first to know."

"Good pup," Rider said. "How about you, Rora?"

"I'm checking in with my entertainment contacts, just in case anyone hears anything on the magic-show front," Rora said.

"Always thinking two steps ahead," Rider said. "Good job."

"*Ssssuddenly, sssso ssssleepy,*" Mr. Meow said with a stretch. "I feel like taking a catnap."

Several others on the police force actually began to snore.

"Hey! What's wrong with these officers?" Ziggy said to Rora. "This

is no time to sleep on the job."

"It's not their fault," Rora said. "It's the fog!"

Beep beep beep! It was Westie's No-Presto Detector again. "Rora's right. That fog is a sleeping gas. It's a Labra trap."

"I'm working on the No-Presto Detector," Westie said, holding up a small device. "It can detect how all illusionist tricks are done."

"They're not called *illusionist* tricks—they're called *magic* tricks!" Ziggy barked. "And that

sounds like a terrible invention! What fun is there in that?"

"Easy, kid," Rora said. "It's a good device to have on our side going up against someone like Labra."

"Why don't we give it a test run?" Westie said. "Care to do a magic trick for us, Ziggy?"

"Sure!" Ziggy stood up from his desk. "See if your No-Fun Detector figures this one out." Suddenly, Ziggy began to levitate—he floated a few inches above the floor.

The No-Presto Detector scanned

Ziggy. *Beep beep beep!*

"According to the No-Presto, you have secret holes in your shoes," Westie explained. "It appears you're floating, but really you're just standing on your tiptoes."

Ziggy growled. "Well, your silly machine won't figure this one out." The young pup grabbed a Styrofoam cup and held it up in one paw. He lifted his other paw

above it and the cup began to float.

"Wow, that's impressive," Rider said. Rora nodded in agreement.

Again, the No-Presto Detector scanned Ziggy. *Beep beep beep!*

"Aha! The No-Presto says you attached a small wire through the back of the cup, so that it appears to float. But it's *you* that's moving it," Westie said.

"That is also impressive," Rider said, clapping Westie on the back.

Ziggy looked sad and deflated.

"Chin up, kid," Rora said. "You fooled me."

Rora's phone rang. At the same time, Ziggy's computer started to light up with new alerts, and Rider's police scanner stated:

"Calling all cars! Calling all cars! There's trouble at Manatee Mike's Magic Emporium!"

Rora grabbed the keys to the P.I. Pack van. "Let's go, boys! I'm driving!"

chapter
FOUR

WELCOME TO THE STAGE

🐾

When the P.I. Pack arrived, the police had Manatee Mike's Magic Emporium surrounded. The mayor and Mr. Meow were there too. It always seemed like Mr. Meow was around when trouble struck.

"What are you doing here, Meow?" Ziggy barked. "And why are you wearing a baby bib?"

"I was having a very delicioussss ssssupper together with the mayor at the new restaurant, the Bee's Knees," Mr. Meow hissed. "Not that it'ssss any of your beessssswax!"

"I never have a night off in this town," said the mayor with a sigh.

"A good dog's work is never done," Rider said, with a tip of his

hat. "What's the situation, sir?"

"Labra-cadabra-dor is inside. He has only one request: He wants to talk to you, Detective . . . alone!"

"Then it looks like I'm going in," Rider said bravely.

"No way! You can't!" Westie and

Ziggy barked at the same time.

"I have to," Rider said. "Wait out here. I'll signal if I need backup." Without a second thought for himself, Rider walked into the magic emporium.

The police stood guard, while the P.I. Pack got on top of their van. Using mini-binoculars that Westie had made, they tried to see inside the shop.

Suddenly, a strange fog floated through the crowd below. The police, the mayor, and Mr. Meow began to yawn.

"The police are okay. They're only sleeping," Rora said. "Now we have to find Rider."

Leaping from car to car, each detective jumped over the fog and made it safely inside the magic shop's front door.

"Not so fast," said a little rabbit, hopping out of the shadows. A
herd of muscle-bound thug bunnies
were right behind him. They all
held magic wands. "No*bunny* moves
unless I tell 'em to. This is Labra's
magic show."

"I may not know much magic," Rora confessed, "but I know a trick—or three." She grabbed a set of silver rings from the shelf and tossed them around three of the bunnies. Then she linked the

rings together
so the bunnies
couldn't escape.
Surprised by
this, the other

rabbits dashed for the exit, but
Westie jumped in their way. "Let's
not fight. Let's shake on it!" He
shook their bunny paws and jolted
them with a joy buzzer.

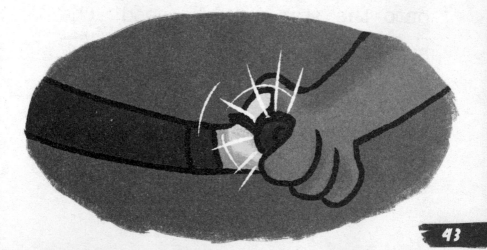

"Okay, that takes care of the the rascally rabbits, but where's Rider?" Rora asked.

Suddenly, a set of red curtains were pulled back to reveal a stage in the store. A spotlight shined on Rider Woofson, who was trapped in a straitjacket and covered in chains.

Labra-cadabra-dor walked out onto the stage. "Ahh, good! The audience finally arrives. And now for a *real* magic show. Lady and gentlepups, I give you . . . the grand finale of Rider Woofson!"

chapter
FIVE

HYPNOTIC HIJINKS

🐾

"Don't worry, team," said Rider with a sly smile. "I've got this crooked magician right where I want him."

"It doesn't look that way, Boss," said Rora.

The P.I. Pack rushed forward to save their friend. "Ah-ah-ah!" Labra said. "I already have my

volunteer for this trick." With a
wave of his wand, Labra magi-
cally lifted ropes off the floor and
tied up the three detectives.

"Don't worry, P.I. Pack," Rider said. "I'm coming!"

Rider began shifting around. His paw appeared with a key, and he began to unlock the chains around him. Then, in almost no time at all, Rider shrugged off the straitjacket. "Time for you to go back to prison, jailbird!"

"Jailbird? I think you mean jail*dog*," Labra said with a smirk. Then he waved his wand again and let out a booming magic word. "LABRA-CADABRA!"

The magician zapped Rider with a powerful beam. Rider stood completely still. His eyes glazed over with spinning black-and-white hypnotized pinwheels.

"When you awaken, you will no longer be Rider Woofson, ace detective," Labra commanded. "Instead you will be Rider Woofson, criminal mastermind and my evil assistant!"

"That will never happen!" Ziggy cried out as he escaped from the magic ropes and leaped onto the

stage. He tried to tackle Labra,
but the magician disappeared in
a cloud of purple-and-gold smoke.

Westie freed himself next with
a handheld laser from his utility
belt. Then he freed Rora, too. They
joined Rider onstage. "Boss,
talk to us!" Westie barked.

Rider shook his head as if waking up, but he had a different look in his eyes. "Who are you? What am I doing here?" he asked.

Another poof of smoke flashed as Labra appeared on the other side of the room surrounded by his henchbunnies. And those rabbits looked mad.

"There's Labra!" yelled Ziggy. "Let's make him vanish—back to prison!"

"I don't think so," Labra said. "Rider, if you don't mind, take care of your friends."

Before Westie or Ziggy knew it, Rider grabbed them by the backs of their shirts. The hypnotized detective flung the two pups into a wooden magician's box. Then an enchanted saw began to cut the box in two.

"Boss, what are you doing?!" Westie cried.

"I never liked this trick!" Ziggy yipped.

"What's going on, Rider?!" Rora shouted as she tried to stop the saw. "They're your friends!"

Rider laughed. "They *were* my friends, but I've got to . . . split.

Henchbunnies, why don't you finish the job?" Suddenly, two henchbunnies grabbed Rora and tossed
her into another magician's box.
Then they locked it shut.

"See you later," Rider sneered.
Then he added, "Not." He left with
Labra as the magician's newest
evil assistant.

chapter
SIX

THE GREAT ESCAPE

🐾

The enchanted saw bit into the box that trapped Westie and Ziggy.

"*This* is why I don't like magic!" yelped Westie as he struggled to escape.

"Well at least this is not an illusion!" snapped Ziggy. "Even though I wish it was!"

"Hold on to your tails, you two,"

Rora called out. "I'm on my way."

She quickly gave the lid a mighty chop. It burst open! Then she raced across the room and stopped the saw before it could finish sawing.

"You saved us!" Ziggy cried.

"Of course I did, kid," Rora said as she threw down the saw.

"Wow! I didn't know you knew Bark-Jitsu!" Westie said.

"I've got even more tricks up these sleeves," Rora said. "But right now, we need to save our boss."

The trio ran outside. Everyone was waking up. There was no sign of Labra or Rider.

"Now what do we do?" Westie whined. "The bunny trail's gone cold!"

"Not necessarily," Rora said.

"I can't imagine the magic-rabbit community is too big in Pawston. Ziggy, maybe your friend Rita Rabbit knows something about Labra and his henchbunnies?"

"*Bow-wowza!* That's a great idea!" Ziggy barked.

After the P.I. Pack made sure the police and the mayor were okay, they hopped into their van and drove to Magic Alley. All the magic-rabbit assistants in Pawston

lived there, including Rita Rabbit. She had three rabbit costumes when she invited the detectives into her home.

"Are those the costumes for our new magic trick, the Bunny Bluff?" asked Ziggy.

"They sure are," said Rita as she handed them to the young pup. "These should fit you three detectives perfectly."

"Unfortunately, we're not here for a magic trick," said Rora. "Do you know anyone who works with Labra-cadabra-dor?"

Rita took two jumps back at the mention of the magician. "All the bunnies in this neighborhood know to stay away from Labra. He's bad news."

"Any chance you know where he's been hiding?" Rora asked.

"I'm sorry," Rita said. "I don't. I wish I could help."

"Thanks, anyway," Rora said. "It looks like we'll need to hit the bricks to find Labra ourselves."

"And thanks for the costumes," said Ziggy.

As they were leaving Rita's den, a special news report sounded on the TV. "This just in!" the reporter said. "There has been a bank

robbery at Pawston First National Bank—and the criminal is the famous detective Rider Woofson! We've just been given the following video of the crime."

The video showed the inside

of an empty bank vault. Without warning, a cloud erupted in the vault, and Rider appeared out of thin air! He looked right at the camera and waved. Then the detective started grabbing everything in sight and shoving the money into a bag. Once he was done, he vanished into another cloud.

The screen switched back to the reporter. "However, Detective Woofson is not the strangest part of this robbery. It appears that the video is dated . . . well, in the *future*! The time stamp on the video is for *tomorrow night*!"

"So what does that mean?" asked Ziggy.

Rora turned off the TV. "It means the

entire city just watched a crime that hasn't been committed yet. And we're going to stop it!"

chapter
SEVEN

NO MAGIC, NO HOW?!

🐾

The P.I. Pack arrived at Pawston First National Bank. There were police everywhere, including their old pal, Frenchie. "Oh, good. P.I. Pack, is Rider with you?"

"No," Rora said. "Labra-cadabra-dor has him trapped under a magic spell."

"Wow! That explains why Rider

robbed the bank," said the police dog. "It doesn't explain why nothing is missing."

"The crime hasn't happened yet," said Rora. "Labra is warning us that it's going to happen tomorrow night."

"Labra would need a time machine for that," Westie argued. "Even *I* can't build a time machine, and I can build anything!"

Frenchie shrugged. "Well, we can't figure out how Rider got into the vault to film the theft. It's like magic, but the video doesn't lie. Maybe you can help?"

The crew inspected the bank,
but they couldn't find any signs
of a break-in. Westie's No-Presto
Detector even said there was no
sign of magic or illusions.

The bank was busy with customers demanding their money

back before Rider could steal it.
The bankers tried to calm the
crowd, but everyone was angry
and scared. They all wanted to
take their money to another bank,
where it would be safe.

"Well, that makes sense," Westie

said. "If they withdraw their money today, then Rider can't steal it tomorrow."

"Hmm, there has to be a logical explanation," Rora said. "Labra wants to ruin Rider's good name. But why didn't he actually steal the money? And why would he show *how* he was going to rob the bank?"

"True. A real magician would never show you how a trick was done," Ziggy said. "Not unless they were using it to perform another trick."

"Wait, what are you talking about?" Rora asked.

"It's called misdirection," Ziggy said. "When a magician gets someone to look in one direction, it's usually because they are doing something secret in another direction."

"That's it!" Rora's eyes lit up. She grabbed Frenchie. "Where are the customers taking their money?"

"Well, there's only one other bank in town," he said. "Pawston Second National Bank."

Rora thanked Frenchie and shuffled the P.I. Pack back to the van. "Let's go, team. I think Labra's magic show is about to start its *final* act."

chapter
EIGHT

Bunnies, Bunnies, Everywhere!

Rora, Westie, and Ziggy zoomed across town to the Pawston Second National Bank.

"I don't get it," Westie said. "Why are we here if the video shows Rider robbing the *First* National Bank? All we need to do is wait for him to show up there tomorrow. Then we undo Labra's spell."

Rora shook her head. "Rider and Labra were never at First National Bank. The target was always Second National."

"Misdirection!" Ziggy said. "I get it now."

"I don't." Westie was confused.

"Can I borrow your X-Ray Binoculars, Westie?" Rora said. He handed over his invention, which could see through walls. Rora stepped out of the van with the others. She used the X-Ray Binoculars to search the area until she found what she was looking for. "There they are!"

Rora handed the binoculars back to Westie. At first he only

saw an empty warehouse behind
the bank. Then he pressed the
X-ray button. Inside the building
he could see a room that looked
exactly like the First National
Bank vault. It was filled with
henchbunnies.

"Okay," said Westie. "I still don't get it."

Rora pointed toward the fake vault. "Rider was never in the actual bank vault, Westie. The video was filmed here and made to *look* like it was in First National

Bank. That way, all the customers would move their money to Second National Bank. Then once all the money was here, Labra was going to rob this bank."

Westie's eyes grew wide as he realized what Rora was saying. "That's like robbing two banks at once! Worst of all, Rider will be blamed for it!"

"I think the robbery is already in progress," Ziggy said, looking through the X-Ray Binoculars. "The henchbunnies have created a door between the warehouse and the Second National Bank vault. As soon as the money goes into the vault, the henchbunnies steal it!"

"What are we going to do?"
Westie asked.

"We are going to rescue Rider
and stop this heist," Rora said.
"Hey, Ziggy. Do you still have those
rabbit costumes? If we want to get
close to Labra, we'll need to look
like some*bunny* else."

No one noticed the three oversize rabbits that snuck into the warehouse and joined the furry crowd.

Rora scanned the room. Rider was helping Labra-cadabra-dor open a garage door. A giant getaway truck was waiting outside with a familiar dog standing next to it.

"Look! It's that rotten rottweiler— Rotten Ruffhouse!" Ziggy whispered.

Rotten waved to Labra and shouted

at the henchbunnies. "Get those lucky rabbit feet hopping and fill up the truck!"

The henchbunnies tossed bags of cash into the truck while Labra and Rotten walked into the warehouse.

Rora grabbed a bag and held it in front of her face so no one could see her. She walked to the truck, put the money in

the back, and ran to the side. Then Rora quietly let the air out of the truck's tires. Her plan was working until someone shouted, "Hey, stop that bunny!"

She'd heard that voice before. It was Rider Woofson!

STAGE SHOWDOWN!

🐾

"Rider, it's me, Rora!" She was still dressed in the bunny costume. "I'm one of the good guys. So are you."

Rider looked confused for a moment. Then he snapped back under Labra's spell.

"Labra!" Rider shouted as he dragged Rora back inside. "Look who I found snooping around. She let the air out of the tires on the getaway truck."

"Good catch," Labra said with a smile.

"Wow, Rider really has turned into one of the bad guys," Rotten said. He seemed impressed. "Wait until my boss hears."

"Who's *your* boss?" Rora asked the rottweiler.

"No*kitty*, er, nobody you know," he said quickly. "Hold on. *I'm* supposed to ask *you* the questions. Where's the rest of the P.I. Pack?"

"Right in front of you!" shouted Westie as he and Ziggy tossed bags of money on Labra and Rotten. Labra fell to the ground,

but Rotten ran away with his tail
between his legs.

Then Rora, Westie, and Ziggy
pulled Rider with them, but they
didn't get very far. Henchbunnies
surrounded the detectives.

"What do we do now?!" Ziggy asked.

"We give these crooks what they want," Rora said. "Bunny money!"

She ripped open a bank bag and tossed it into the air. Cash flew everywhere. As the henchbunnies tried to nab the money, the P.I. Pack yanked Rider toward another exit. They had almost escaped when Rider grabbed a mirror that was by the door.

"I'm not going anywhere with you," he said coldly.

"Come on, Boss. Snap out of

it!" Rora demanded. "And why are you holding that mirror?"

"So *I* can do *this*," Labra said from behind them. The magician zapped a beam that bounced off the mirror. Rora turned away just in time, but the spell captured Westie and Ziggy. They were hypnotized just like Rider!

Rora was all alone. She looked around the room. Labra and his henchbunnies were in front of her. Rider and her spellbound friends were behind her. On her left and right sides were boxes of items used in magic

shows, like lights, curtains, and a
silver disco ball. Rora smiled. She
had an idea.

"Please, make this easy on your-
self," Labra said. "Surrender now
and become one of my assistants."

"No way, you crook! I would rather disappear!" Rora shouted.

"We can make that happen," Labra said as he raised the magic wand and fired another spell.

But Rora was too fast. She

grabbed the disco ball from its box and held it up like a shield. The magic beam struck the disco ball and reflected all around the room. The spell dazzled, shined, and hypnotized everyone in its path, including Labra-cadabra-dor.

Rora put down the ball and walked up to the evil magician. "Labra, as *my* personal assistant, I command you to free my friends from your spell."

chapter TEN

THE <u>MAGIC</u> WORD

🐾

Rider felt like he was just waking up from a dog nap. His friends were leaning over him. "What . . . what happened? And why are you all dressed like bunnies?"

"Rora saved the day," Westie said.

"And gave Labra a taste of his own medicine!" Ziggy added.

Rider stood up and studied the crooked yet blank-faced magician. "Good job, Rora. What should we do with him now? It's wrong to keep him under the spell forever."

"I've got an idea," Rora said with a smile. She whispered something in Labra's ear. Then she snapped her fingers, and he woke up.

"You are under arrest," Rora said. She snatched his wand and broke it in half.

"No! My precious wand!" Labra cried.

"Don't worry," Rider said. "You can keep doing magic—in your prison cell."

As soon as Rider said the word "magic," Labra started to act like a chicken. He flapped his arms like wings, kicked his legs, and said, *"Bawk! Bawk! BAWK!"*

"What did you do to him?" Rider asked.

Rora smiled. "I used his own spell against him. Now anytime he hears the word 'magic,' he'll act like a chicken."

Sure enough, when Rora said the word "magic," Labra started to act like a chicken again. Everyone laughed.

"Thank you, Rora," Rider said. "You didn't just save my career— you saved me from a life of crime."

"Just doing my job, Boss," she said.

The P.I. Pack walked Labra outside and put him in the back of

a police officer's car. "Take this chicken to jail!" Rora said.

"Yes, ma'am!" the driver said as he drove away.

A few blocks later, the police car turned off the road into a private driveway.

"Where are we going?" Labra asked. "This isn't the way to The Cage."

"That's right," the police officer said, taking off his hat and sunglasses. It was Rotten Ruffhouse.

"I'm taking you to meet the boss."

Labra stepped out of the car to find Mr. Meow waiting for him. "I have an offer for you, my criminal friend."

"I work alone," Labra told the cat. "I'm more of a solo act."

"Of course. Though, perhaps we could share the evil stage as part-nerssss," Mr. Meow suggested.

"Maybe," Labra said. "What did you have in mind?"

Mr. Meow clicked his claws together. "I want to get rid of that infernal Rider Woofsssson and his dog detectivessss forever."

"Sounds like *magic* . . . ," Labra said, though as soon as he spoke the "magic" word, he instantly regretted it.

CHECK OUT RIDER WOOFSON'S NEXT CASE!

"Welcome to the Catskills History Museum. My name is Tina, and I'll be your tour guide. If you have any questions, just ask!"

Tina led the tourists through the museum. The first exhibit was dinosaur skeletons. "This pre-historic moment shows dino-dogs and cat-osaurs. Though they may look like cats and dogs, they were actually more closely related to birds!"

The next exhibit showed proud animals in togas. "This is the Roaming Period," Tina explained. "The Dog-Run Maximus, Juli*hiss* Caesar, and Salamander the Great are just a few classic heroes of their time. They roamed and ruled over many different lands. Now, if you'll follow me to the next exhibit, I can tell you the story of King Arthur and the sword*fish* in the stone."

"Oooh, what's that?" a tourist asked. They pointed at a WANTED CRIMINAL poster.

"That is the international art thief known as the Big Bad Woof," said Tina. "Not much is known about the dangerous crook except that he steals valuable works of art. But this poster is not part of the tour—"

Excerpt from *The Big Bad Woof*